Simon and the Snow

D1361412

For Claudia

First published in Great Britain in 1987 by Hutchinson Children's Books
An imprint of Century Hutchinson Ltd
Brookmount House, 62–65 Chandos Place,
Covent Garden, London WC2N 4NW

Century Hutchinson Australia (Pty) Ltd
16-22 Church Street, Hawthorn, Melbourne, Victoria 3122

Century Hutchinson New Zealand Limited
32–34 View Road, PO Box 40–086, Glenfield, Auckland 10

Century Hutchinson South Africa (Pty) Ltd
PO Box 337, Bergvlei 2012, South Africa

Set in Goudy Old Style Roman

Printed and bound in Italy by Grafiche AZ/Verona

British Library Cataloguing in Publication Data

Alberti, Gino
   Simon and the snow.
   1. Title 2. Wolfsgruber, Sieglinde
   3. Simon und die Tiere. *English*
   833'.914[J]   PZ7

ISBN 0-09-172674-3

Simon and the Snow

Gino Alberti and Sieglinde Wolfsgruber

HUTCHINSON

London   Melbourne   Auckland   Johannesburg

Simon lived in a little house high up in the mountains. It was winter and he was happy, for of all the seasons he loved winter the best.

He loved the snowflakes and the icicles; he loved to take long rides on his sledge, and most of all he loved to build jolly round snowmen with carrot noses.

One day Simon looked around him and noticed grass growing and new buds on the trees. Spring had come early.

Simon was sad: he wished it could be winter for ever.

But that night, as Simon lay sleeping, the air turned cold again. Softly, it began to snow. The garden was covered in white and the windows were speckled with frost.

As soon as Simon woke up, he noticed that something was different. He ran to the window and looked out in wonder at the snow. The winter had come back again! It was as if his wish had come true.

'The snow is back! The snow is back!' he cried out joyfully. He put on his woolly hat and mittens and ran outside. He began to build a whole family of snowmen. His mother gave him some carrots for the noses and some straw for the arms. Simon was very happy.

The next day was even colder. As soon as he was up, Simon went to play with his snow family. But what had happened? He ran from one snowman to the next. The twig arms and the carrot noses were gone! Who could have done such a thing?

There was no time to think for Simon's mother was calling him in to breakfast. Later, as Simon fetched some new noses and arms from the kitchen, he made a plan.

That night the sky was so clear you could count the stars. While his mother slept, Simon, wrapped up warmly, collected his cat Mutz and climbed out through the window. Together they trudged through the snow until they came to a very tall tree. 'Here's a good place,' said Simon as he climbed up. Mutz followed. They were cold and frightened, but even if they had to stay up all night they would catch the carrot thieves.

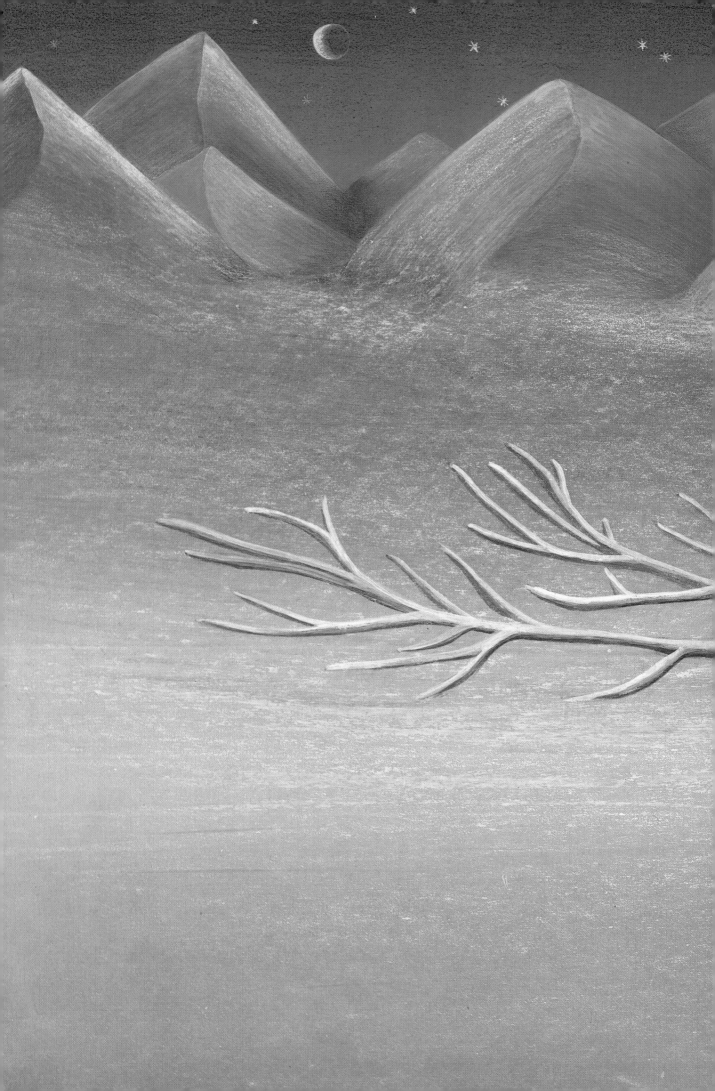

For a long, long while everything was still. Then, suddenly, Simon saw something move. Gathering up his courage he climbed down the tree and hid behind a snowman. He could hardly believe his eyes – all kinds of animals were coming out of the forest and they were greedily eating everything they could from the snowmen.

Simon could see that the poor animals were very thin and hungry. The return of the winter had buried their food under deep snow. He quietly took a couple of steps towards them, but the animals ran away in fright.

Later that morning, Simon told his mother what had happened. 'The poor animals are starving,' she said, and she gave him a basket of hay to take to them.

Simon carried the basket to the edge of the forest. The animals gazed at him hungrily. 'Don't be frightened,' Simon whispered.

Very, very slowly a little deer dared to come forward. Then, when the other animals saw it was safe, they too came out of the forest. There were fawns and rabbits and stags and birds. Simon fed as many as he could, but there wasn't enough food for everyone. Then Simon had an idea.

He put the basket on his back and set off to the village. Shyly, the animals followed him. The village people stopped what they were doing to watch the strange little procession making its way down the mountain.

Everyone wanted to hear Simon's story. He told them about his snowmen and how he had discovered the hungry animals. The whole village wanted to help. At the entrance to the village the grown-ups built a big feeding trough. Then all the children ran home to fetch food for the animals.

Every day, the children brought new supplies. There was enough for all.

Soon the snow melted and the days began to grow warmer. The smell of new grass was in the air again. Spring had come at last – this time to stay. The animals could go back to the forest for good.

From that time on, Simon still loved the winter, but now he loved the spring as well, for he knew the importance of the seasons.